Davy Crockett

YOUNG PIONEER

By Laurence Santrey and
JoAnn Early Macken
Illustrated by Francis Livingston

SCHOLASTIC INC.
New York   Toronto   London   Auckland   Sydney
Mexico City   New Delhi   Hong Kong   Buenos Aires

ISBN-13: 978-0-439-02048-0
ISBN-10: 0-439-02048-4

12 11 10 9 8 7 6 5 4 3 2   8 9 10 11 12 13/0

Printed in the U.S.A.
First printing, January 2008

Davy Crockett

YOUNG PIONEER

CONTENTS

Davy Crockett

YOUNG PIONEER

CHAPTER 1:
A Person and a Legend

In the 1950s, a TV series based on the life of Davy Crockett called him the "King of the Wild Frontier." After watching the Walt Disney Productions special, millions of American children wore raccoon skin caps and sang the program's theme song. The song, which said that Davy killed a bear when he was only three, was a national hit for thirteen weeks!

Who was Davy Crockett? He was a real person, born on August 17, 1786. Many stories are told about him. Some are truthful, some are exaggerated, and some are truly tall tales. Davy Crockett himself added to the folklore. He wrote a book, published in 1834, called *A Narrative of the Life of David Crockett of the State of Tennessee.* Its colorful language gives us clues to the kind of person he must have been.

Davy's mother, Rebecca Hawkins, was born in Maryland. Davy's father, John Crockett, came to America from Ireland when he was a baby. He grew up in Pennsylvania and fought in the Revolutionary War. He also lived in North Carolina before moving to the territory that became Tennessee. There, he hunted for food for his family, and worked as a constable.

In Tennessee, Davy's family lived in a log cabin near Limestone Creek. The creek flowed into the Nolichucky River. The cabin was made of oak, and the windows were oiled paper. Davy, the fifth of nine children, had five brothers and three sisters. He was named David after his grandfather Crockett.

Davy's parents were hardworking pioneers. They had to plow the fields, plant and harvest the crops, milk the cows, and feed their growing family. After he grew up, Davy is said to have joked about his parents this way:

"My daddy is a true sample of white oak. His bark's a little wrinkled, but his trunk is so all flinty hard that you can strike fire from it with a sledgehammer. He can still look the sun in the face without sneezing. He can still grin a hailstorm into sunshine.

"My maw, she's a glorious girl for her age. She can still jump a seven-rail fence backward, dance a hole through a double oak floor, spin more wool than one of your steam mills, and smoke a bale of Kentucky tobacco in her corncob pipe in a week. She can crack walnuts for her great-grandchildren with her front teeth and laugh a horse blind. She can cut down a gum tree ten feet around and steer it across Salt River with her apron for a sail and her left leg for a rudder."

Tales about Davy say he was about the biggest, smartest baby ever born. "Because of his size," one story says, "Davy was given an oversize cradle made from the shell of an oversize snapping turtle. His pillow was a wildcat skin filled with the down from thirty-three geese and eleven ganders."

Other stories describe Davy's great appetite. One tells how he sometimes ate a whole duck and a big helping of bear meat for a meal. A snack was a sandwich made of "half a bear's hind leg and two spareribs in a loaf of bread." Young Davy was said to like his bear meat "fixed just right—salted in a hailstorm, peppered with buckshot, and broiled on a flash of forked lightning."

CHAPTER 2:
Danger on the River!

Davy Crockett describes one of his earliest memories in his book. One day, five of the Crockett boys and a fifteen-year-old friend named Campbell played on the bank of the Nolichucky River. Not far away, a large waterfall crashed to the river below.

Davy's four older brothers climbed into Mr. Crockett's canoe with the Campbell boy, leaving Davy alone on the shore. The four-year-old did not like being left behind, but he could do nothing about it. So he stood on the bank and howled. He never forgot what happened next.

"My brothers, though they were little fellows, had been used to paddling the canoe and could have carried it safely anywhere about there. But this fellow Campbell wouldn't let them have the paddle, but fool like, undertook to manage it himself. I reckon he had never seen a watercraft before, and it went just any way but the way he wanted it. He paddled and paddled and paddled—all the while going wrong—until, in a short time, here they were all going straight forward, stern foremost, right plump to the falls, and if they had only a fair shake, they would have gone over as slick as a whistle."

A farmer working in a nearby field heard Davy yell and looked up to see the canoe heading for the falls. He ran for the water, tearing off his coat and his shirt on the way. Seeing the man running toward him in such a

hurry scared Davy even more, so he screamed
again. The man dove into the river to rescue
the boys. He splashed through the water as
fast as he could. By the time he reached the
boys, they were only twenty or thirty feet
from the falls.

The farmer lunged forward and grabbed

the canoe. The current was so strong that the man could barely stop the canoe. But he held on until it stopped, and then he pulled it out of danger. "When they got out," Davy said, "I found the boys were more scared than I had been, and the only thing that comforted me was the belief that it was a punishment on them for leaving me onshore."

CHAPTER 3:
Young Hunter

When he was six years old, one story says, Davy had a big, woolly dog named Butcher. Davy rode around on Butcher's back "faster than lightning splitting a post." The dog barked at bears and chased after them. Davy shot the ones that could not get away and hide.

Though perhaps not at six years old, Davy must have started hunting when he was quite young. He might have learned how from his father or his brothers. His uncle Joseph Hawkins also may have taken him out hunting. Davy would have had to learn

a great deal before he could safely hunt on
his own. He had to know how to find his way
home from the woods. He learned the noises
of the animals that prowled the forests. In the
winter, he had to listen for the sounds of the
river-ice cracking so he could tell whether it
was safe to cross. He knew how his dogs acted
when they chased a bear. He could tell how
tall a bear was by studying the claw marks it
made on trees. And he had to learn how to
use a gun.

One day, a story claims, Davy's family needed food. Davy was so busy with chores that he hardly had time to hunt. He carried a double-barreled shotgun to the river, where he saw a flock of geese and a huge deer. He waited until they were close together so he could shoot them all at once. Just as he raised the gun, he saw a rattlesnake. With one barrel, he shot the deer. With the other, he shot the whole line of geese. He killed the snake with the ramrod, a tool used to shove an explosive charge into a gun muzzle. The gun kicked so hard that Davy fell into the river, where his pockets filled up with fish. His coat was so heavy then that the buttons popped off, killing a squirrel and a bear. He finished his hunting in a hurry that day.

In 1794, when Davy was almost eight years old, the Crocketts moved to Cove Creek, Tennessee. Mr. Crockett and a partner bought a plot of land right next to the creek. It seemed

a perfect place to build a mill. The settlers pouring into the area would all need a place to take their grain to be ground into flour.

Davy's father and older brothers had to build a waterwheel, set up the grindstone, and build the family's home above the mill. Winter passed and, by spring, the work was nearly done.

Then the spring rains came, swelling the creek. The water rose higher and higher, flooding the mill. Soon, the water reached the second floor, where the family lived. The Crocketts had to rush out of the house and hurry to higher ground. The mill and their home were totally lost. Gathering everything worth saving, the Crocketts left Cove Creek forever.

Davy's father moved the family to a small country inn. It stood next to the road between Abingdon, Virginia, and Knoxville, Tennessee. Hunters, trappers, settlers, and other travelers passed by on their way back and forth. The inn had room for the family and a few paying guests.

Mrs. Crockett cooked for the family and guests and took care of the younger children. Mr. Crockett and the older children served the guests, fed and stabled their horses, and raised vegetables. Davy helped with the chores and hunted for food for everyone. He lived this way for the next few years.

18

CHAPTER 4:
Four Hundred Miles from Home

When Davy was twelve, a farmer named Jacob Siler stopped at the inn on his way to Virginia. He was driving a herd of cattle, and he found it difficult to manage the cattle by himself. Mr. Siler asked Mr. Crockett if one of the Crockett boys could travel with him. Mr. Siler said he would pay the boy a fair wage. Mr. Crockett asked Davy to go. Davy hardly knew the man, but he agreed.

The next morning, Mr. Siler and Davy

started their four-hundred-mile trip. Davy says in his book that he set out "with a heavy heart." He walked every step of the way, keeping the cattle from straying or getting lost. When he reached the Virginia farm, Davy received five dollars. Mr. Siler told Davy he was pleased with the boy's work.

Then Mr. Siler told Davy he wanted him to stay on the farm and work as a hired hand. Davy really wanted to go home, but he remembered that Mr. Crockett had told him to obey Mr. Siler. Although the boy was homesick, he wanted to do as his father had told him. He stayed. One record says he was "about twice as unhappy as a kitten in a cold creek."

A month or so later, Davy was playing with some other boys on the side of a road near the farm. Three wagons rolled past. They belonged to Mr. Dunn, a man from Tennessee, and his two sons. Mr. Dunn

was a regular visitor at Davy's father's inn. The three men were headed for Knoxville. On the way, they planned to stop at the inn again.

Davy told the man why he was there, how much he missed his family, and that he wanted to go home. After Mr. Dunn heard the story, he told Davy it would be all right for him to go back to Tennessee. Even so, Davy was afraid to tell Mr. Siler he was leaving. He decided he would have to sneak away from the farm.

"We're staying at the inn seven miles down this road," Mr. Dunn told Davy. "We'll be leaving for Tennessee at dawn tomorrow. If you get there before then, I'll take you home."

Davy went back to the Siler farm. The family was out visiting. Davy gathered his clothes and what little money he had. He went to bed early, but he could not sleep. He kept thinking of his family and he was afraid he would be caught sneaking out.

About three hours before sunrise, Davy left the Siler farm. Snow was falling heavily, and nearly eight inches of white powder already covered the ground. The falling snow filled the night sky, blocking any moonlight. Davy had to guess where the road ran between the trees.

By the time Davy reached Mr. Dunn's
wagon, the snow was up to his knees. He
was happy to see that he hadn't left any
tracks. With an hour to go before daybreak,
he had walked seven miles in deep snow
and darkness. He was exhausted and almost
frozen, but he could not have been happier.
Mr. Dunn welcomed the boy, fed him some
breakfast, and sent him to warm himself by
the fire. A short while later, the Dunns, their

three wagons, and Davy set out on their journey to Tennessee.

The closer he got to home, the more eager Davy grew. He was glad to rest in the wagon, but the ride was slow and bumpy. One morning, he decided to walk, thinking he could go faster on foot. As he walked, a man on horseback caught up to him. The man had an extra horse, and he asked Davy if he wanted to ride it. Davy gladly took the ride, which meant he did not have to wade or swim across the cold river. He rode with the man until he was fifteen miles from home. Then he walked the rest of the way. His family was as delighted to see Davy as he was to be back home.

CHAPTER 5:
Hard Lessons

Davy, who by this time had turned thirteen, stayed around home, hunting and helping with the chores. Then Mr. Crockett decided his children should get some education—the first schooling for any of them. A man named Benjamin Kitchen ran a country school in a log cabin down the road from the Crockett home.

Davy went to school for four whole days. In that time, he began to learn to read and write the alphabet. One afternoon, he got into a fight with a classmate on the way home from school. After the fight, which Davy won, he knew he was in trouble. Mr. Kitchen did not allow fighting, and Davy expected to be punished.

The next morning, when the Crockett boys left for school, Davy went only part of the way with his brothers. He asked them not to tell their father, and then he spent the day in the woods. He did the same thing for several days. Finally, Mr. Kitchen sent a note to Mr. Crockett, asking why Davy had been absent.

Mr. Crockett had a talk with Davy. When he learned why the boy was skipping school, Mr. Crockett said, "Make your choice, Davy. If you go to school, you'll get a whipping from your teacher. If you don't go, you'll get a worse one from me."

Davy did not like either choice. He ran out of the house with his father on his heels. He

ran down the road away from the school. His father was a little slower, though. As Davy crested the top of a hill, he turned and hid in the bushes. His father passed by without seeing him, gave up, and returned home.

Davy thought the best thing to do was to leave for a while, until his father and Mr. Kitchen both had had a chance to cool down. He took a job with a man who was driving a herd of cattle to Virginia. Davy's older brother went along. When they got to the end of the trail, Davy was paid four dollars and was told he was on his own.

Davy thought about going home, but he could not forget the way he had left Mr. Kitchen and his father. "I was afraid to venture back," he said, "for I knew my father's nature so well that I was certain his anger would hang on to him like a turtle does to a fisherman's toe."

Davy's brother tried to talk him into going home, but Davy refused. Instead, he looked for another job.

CHAPTER 6:

Job After Job

One story calls a farm where Davy worked "about the poorest place that was ever made. When killdeers flew over this place, the tears came to their eyes so they could hardly see. The apples were pitiful little runts of things so sour they made the pigs that ate them howl. The hound dogs were so poor they had to lean against a fence before they could bark."

Davy worked for one farmer for twenty-five cents a day. He earned enough money to buy some new clothes. A wagoner had

promised to take him back to Tennessee, but the man could not find a load to haul that way. Instead, he was driving to Baltimore with a load of flour in barrels. Davy decided to go with him. He gave the wagoner his money to hold, about seven dollars.

Along the way, the wagon broke down. While it was being fixed, Davy wandered to the wharf to see the huge sailing ships. He snuck aboard a ship to explore. The captain told Davy the ship was leaving for London that night. He asked Davy to work for him, and Davy agreed to take the job. Davy went back to the wagoner to pick up his money and clothes, but the wagoner refused to let Davy go.

The man would not let Davy out of his sight. After a few days, Davy packed his clothes. He waited until the man was asleep, and then he left, even though he had no money. Along the road, he met another wagoner who tried to help him get his money back. The first man confessed that he had spent Davy's money and could not pay him back.

Davy traveled with the second wagoner for a few days and then decided to try to go home. First, he spent a night at a place where several other wagoners stayed. After they heard his story, the men collected some money for Davy. He left with three dollars.

By the time that money ran out, Davy had made it as far as Virginia. He worked at one job after another, each time saving enough money to travel a little farther. Davy worked for a farmer for a month and earned five dollars. Then for eighteen months, he worked for a hatmaker, who lost all his money and left the country. Davy was left with nothing, and even his clothes were worn out. He tried once again to make his way home.

Close to home, he reached a river so rough

that no one would take him across. He begged until someone let him borrow a canoe. He tied his clothes to the canoe to keep from losing them. The wind was so strong that he paddled nearly two miles before he could land. By the time he reached the other side, he was soaked, and the canoe was half full of water. At last, Davy reached his brother's house in Tennessee. Davy stayed there for a few weeks. Then he headed for home.

CHAPTER 7:

Home at Last

Late one evening, Davy walked into the Crocketts' inn and asked if he could stay there for the night. As he remembered later, "I had been gone so long, and had grown so much, that the family did not at first know me. And another, and perhaps a stronger reason was they had no thought or expectation of me, for they all had long given me up for finally lost.

"After a while, we were all called to supper. I went with the rest. We had all sat down to

the table and began to eat, when my eldest
sister recollected me. She sprung up, ran and
seized me around the neck, and exclaimed,
'Here is my lost brother!'"

The family was so glad to see Davy that he
was sorry he had stayed away so long. When
he found out how much they had missed
him, he wished he had taken his punishment
and gone back to school. He learned that his
family had not heard a word about him since
he left his brother in Virginia. By this time,
he was almost fifteen.

After he stayed with his family for a while,
he learned that his father owed thirty-six
dollars to Abraham Wilson, a local farmer.
Mr. Crockett asked Davy to work for the
farmer until the debt was paid. After six
months of hard work without a single day
off, Davy gave his father a piece of paper that
declared the debt paid in full.

A short time later, Davy went to work for a man named John Kennedy. There, he learned that his father owed this man forty dollars. Without being asked, Davy decided to work off this debt, too. He worked there for six months. Even though it was only fifteen miles from home, he never went back until the debt was paid. Then he borrowed a horse to go give his father the good news. After that, he went back to work. Once again, he needed some new clothes.

After a few months, John Kennedy's niece came for a visit, and Davy fell in love. He was so nervous, he said, that "when I would think of saying anything to her, my heart would begin to flutter like a duck in a puddle, and if I tried to outdo it and speak, would get right smack up in my throat and choke me like a cold potato."

When he found out the girl was engaged, he was crushed. He wondered if something was wrong with him. He thought that maybe all his troubles came from his lack of learning. He made up his mind to go back to school.

CHAPTER 8:

West to the Wilderness

Davy made a deal with a local school teacher. Davy would go to school four days a week and work for the teacher two days a week. Davy also asked for meals and a place to stay. Over the next six months, the teacher taught Davy to read, write, and do a little arithmetic. That was all the formal education Davy ever had. Then he decided it was time to find a wife.

"So I cut out to hunt one," he says in his book, as if he were looking for wild game. "I

42

found a pretty little girl that I'd known since I was very young. . . . I got to feeling I'd fight a whole regiment of wildcats if she would say she'd have me." He learned from her sister that she also planned to marry someone else. "This was as sudden to me as a clap of thunder on a bright sunshiny day," he says. He was miserable for weeks.

At last, at a dance, he met Polly Finley. They talked, ate, and danced until nearly dawn. Davy had to keep seeing her. He decided he needed a horse, so he worked for six more months to earn it. Whenever he could, he rode to visit Polly.

In August 1806, Davy and Polly were married at the Finley home. The next day, they had a reception at the Crockett family's inn.

Davy had his horse and his rifle. Polly had a spinning wheel, and she was a good weaver. The Finleys gave the couple two cows and their calves. A friend gave them fifteen dollars to buy what they needed. They rented a farm and a cabin.

Within three years, Polly and Davy had two sons, John Wesley and William Finley. Farming their land was not easy, so they decided to move. They packed their goods on their horses and headed west. They lived for two years near the Mulberry Fork of the Elk River. From there, they moved to a place called Bean Creek. In 1812, their daughter, Margaret Finley, was born.

Tall tales were told about the other Crocketts, too. One writer described the family this way: "Davy's wife was a streak of lightning set up edgeways and buttered with quicksilver. She could blow out the moonlight and sing a wolf to sleep. The children were what you'd expect: They could outrun, outjump, and outscream almost any creature in creation. They could also outfight a middling-size thunderstorm."

In the wilderness, Davy earned his reputation as a hunter. He could track any animal, and with old Betsy, his trusty rifle, he brought down raccoons, bears, and deer. Davy himself boasted that he killed 105 bears in less than a year. Word of Davy's skill spread, and the legends that grew around him became part of America's folklore. Stories say that he tamed an alligator, a panther, a wolf, and a bear, and taught them all how to do chores.

Davy's fame grew even greater as a scout under General Andrew Jackson in the War of 1812. But he returned home from war to find Polly sick. She died, leaving him with three small children. Davy soon married a widow, Elizabeth Patton, who already had two children. A short time later, Davy left to hunt and explore the frontier. He came down with malaria and was bedridden for two weeks. Elizabeth had heard that he died, so she was shocked—and, of course, happy—to see him come home.

Together, Davy and Elizabeth had three more children. The growing family moved farther west near Shoal Creek. There, Davy began to get involved in politics. In 1821, he was elected to the U.S. Congress. In a speech to Congress, he said, "I've got the roughest racking horse, the prettiest sister, the surest rifle, and the ugliest dog in the district. My father can whip any man in Tennessee, and I can lick my father. I can give any man on this floor two hours' start and outspeak him. I can run faster, dive deeper, stay under longer, and come up drier than any man this side of the Big Swamp. I can outgrin a panther and outstare a flash of lightning, tote a steamboat on my back and play at rough and tumble with a lion, with a kick now and then from a zebra."

Davy was known in Congress for his positions on two issues. He believed that settlers who cleared land should be able to buy it for a low price. And he refused to vote for a bill that forced Indians off their land.

Davy Crockett's greatest fame came for his part in the defense of the Alamo, a fort in San Antonio, Texas. There, a small band of soldiers fought a long battle for the independence of Texas. They held out as long as they could, before being overrun by the huge Mexican army, led by General Antonio López de Santa Anna.

On March 6, 1836, the great pioneer and patriot died along with the other brave defenders of the Alamo. Davy Crockett was only forty-nine years old. But in his short lifetime, he carved a legend of skill and courage that will live forever.

Index

Look for these other exciting
EASY BIOGRAPHIES: